JEAN ROGERS

Raymond's Best Summer

pictures by MARYLIN HAFNER

Greenwillow Books
New York

Library of Congress Cataloging-in-Publication Data
Rogers, Jean.
Raymond knows best / by Jean Rogers ;
pictures by Marylin Hafner.
                  p.   cm.
Summary: Raymond's boring summer becomes exciting
as he learns how to swim and helps the police catch
a gang of thieves burglarizing the neighborhood.
ISBN 0-688-09391-4
[1. Swimming—Fiction.   2. Summer—Fiction.]
I. Hafner, Marylin, ill.   II. Title.
PZ7.R6355Ray   1990
[Fic]—dc20   89–34772   CIP   AC

To Susan, Libby, and Ava

1

Pemberton Elementary School had been closed for a whole week when the Kenton Municipal Swimming Pool opened. Swimming classes began that very day, and Raymond and his friends Benjamin, Eloise, and Kim were all signed up for lessons.

When Raymond's mother called up the stairs to hurry him along, he was all ready to grab his swim bag and go. Eloise and Kim were just coming across the street as he and his mother got into the Wayliss car. Before they could back out of the drive, Benjamin came running around the corner.

The municipal pool was at the other end of town, so each of the mothers had agreed to take turns driving. Raymond was pleased that his mother was driving that first day.

"Be sure to fasten your seat belts," he said importantly to his friends in the back seat. "I'm the copilot, and it's my job to check the passengers in."

Eloise snorted. "Did you fasten your own seat belt?"

"I do mine after I've checked on everyone else," Raymond answered huffily, but he quickly turned around and snapped his shoulder strap into locked position. "All clear," he said to his mother.

Mrs. Wayliss waited until they were all

checked in at the pool and assigned to a class. "Isn't this nice," she said approvingly. "You're all in the same group. I'm going now, but I'll be back for you right at twelve o'clock. Have a good time."

Raymond and Benjamin headed for the boys' dressing room while Eloise and Kim went off to the girls' side. They met again beside the big pool with the other children in their class.

"My name is Lori, and I'm your teacher," said a young woman. She had a gym whistle on a cord around her neck and a clipboard in her hand.

First she handed each one of them a red plastic tag to tie onto his or her swimsuit. Other classes, each clustered around a teacher, stood in groups around the pool. Raymond noticed that the team closest to his group was being given yellow tags. He didn't see anyone else from Pemberton School. He was happy to see that his special friends were all together on the team he already thought of as his. Red was the best color, too.

That first morning simply flew by. Lori led them into the water at the shallow end of the pool. She asked them all to splash a bit and then to put their faces right down into the water.

"Wonderful, that's great," she cried. "Not one of you was afraid! What a good class! I'll have you swimming in no time at all."

The rest of the morning Lori continued to tell them what a smart class they were. They were great kickers, great splashers, and great jumpers. "I've never had a quicker class," she said, beaming.

Before class was over, she gave them time to practice ducking their heads underwater without holding their noses. She smiled approvingly when every single one of them could do it. Raymond was always the very last one to raise his head from the water, and Lori said he had wonderful breath control.

Raymond and Benjamin were showered, dried, dressed, and waiting out front for a while before Eloise and Kim joined them.

"I'll bet I can swim by tomorrow," Eloise boasted. "I can already float a little all by myself. I could do that last summer when we went on our trip. Daddy just needed one finger to hold me up. We never stopped at a motel that didn't have a pool, and Daddy said if we just had another week of traveling, I'd have learned how to swim for sure."

None of the others made any promises to swim by tomorrow, but they all agreed swimming lessons were fun and tomorrow couldn't come too soon.

2

It took two more lessons before Eloise could really float by herself. "Look at me!" she shouted, and promptly went under. She came up choking and sputtering but immediately stretched out again, and sure enough, she was floating.

"Oh great!" Lori called. "Eloise, that's marvelous. You're the very first one. Come on, Red Team, that's how you do it. I know you all can do it, too. I want you all floating just like that by the end of the week."

Raymond was determined to be the next one to float. Over and over again he lay back in the water and relaxed, holding his breath. He did it exactly as Lori told him, but he couldn't stop himself from rolling over onto his stomach. His feet would begin to sink, and though he could hold his breath a wonderfully long time, somehow he always turned right over.

Lori said that was a good way to float as well. She told everyone to try it. She had Raymond show them how easy it was. The entire class could float that way, too, but no one could stay facedown in the water as long as Raymond. Yet though he tried and tried, he couldn't float on his back.

"Maybe you're not relaxed enough," Lori said, watching him closely. "Just go limp all over," she suggested. After Raymond tried some more, she said she couldn't see why he didn't stay on his back. "You're sure doing everything right. But don't sweat it, Raymond. Just do your own thing. Back or front, floating is floating."

On Friday Lori said, "Goodbye till Monday, kids. I know you're all going to be absolutely wonderful swimmers. Red Team is the best." She gave them all a big smile.

The next week they concentrated on learning how to kick. They held on to the side of the pool and kicked as hard as they could. They made grand and glorious splashes. Very soon Lori said they were the best flutter-kickers she had ever seen. "Right on!" she cried. She didn't mind a bit that she was splashed all over as she watched them from the side of the pool. It was fun for everyone.

Presently Lori gave them each a Styrofoam square to hold on to while they kicked. "Boy,"

Benjamin shouted to Raymond, "this is really like swimming." Raymond agreed. He felt sure Lori was right. Everyone on Red Team, *his* class, was going to be an exceptional swimmer.

By the end of that week—the week Eloise had copiloted them, checking seat belts and making a big fuss over her job—all of the Red Team were accomplished kickers and thrashers. "You're all so much at home in the water," Lori said on Friday. "Monday we'll be ready to go for it. Yea, team!"

Mrs. Ellsworth, Kim's mother, drove Monday morning. Scott's car seat took up a lot of space in the back seat. Raymond and Benjamin were barely able to squeeze in beside him. Kim and Eloise both sat in front. They were so busy tucking themselves under the one seat belt there that Kim didn't issue any orders to the boys in the back at all.

At the pool Lori had them all line up and jump in the water as usual. "But when you come up," she directed, "I want you to try swimming across the pool. Get as far as you can, and when you have to stop, stand right there so I can see how far you made it. Just paddle your arms the way I showed you. It doesn't matter how far you get. Just stop when you need to. Remember to kick hard, okay?"

She blew her whistle, and Red Team leaped into the pool. Raymond kicked as hard as he could and swung his arms. Before he ran out of breath, he bumped into the opposite wall and clawed his way up for air. He had come completely across the pool without needing to breathe. He was pleased with himself and looked around to see how the others were doing. They all were still trying to thrash their way across the pool or had already stopped, standing in place as Lori had told them to.

As beginners the class was not yet in deep water. They were trying to swim across the pool, not down its length, but Raymond was the only one standing on the opposite side. "Raymond," Lori called, "what are you doing over there? I didn't see you swimming at all."

"Well, I did," answered Raymond. "I held my breath and here I am."

"Swim on over," Lori said to the rest of the class, "and climb out. When I blow the whistle, jump in and try coming back across."

When the others joined him, Raymond did exactly as he had done before. Taking a deep breath, he plunged in and bumped into the wall before he needed to come up for air. Once again he was the only one to make it completely across. Lori looked down at him with a very puzzled expression on her face.

"How did you get here? I must have lost you in all the splashers." It was clear to Raymond, Lori didn't think he could swim all that way.

"Want me to do it again?" he asked eagerly.

"Okay, hop in and show us, Raymond." One of the girls made a move to jump in also. "No, Lynn," Lori said, "I want the rest of you to stay out a minute."

Confidently Raymond jumped into the water for the third time. When he bumped into the side of the pool as he had done before, he popped up, smiling. This was great fun.

"Why, Raymond," Lori called over to him, "what *were* you doing? Were you crawling along the bottom or were you actually swimming?"

Raymond didn't know what she meant. He

had pumped his arms and kicked his legs exactly as she had said to do. He certainly hadn't been crawling. He must have been swimming.

Without saying a word he climbed out of the pool and jumped in once more. He kicked harder than ever and paddled his arms furiously. When he felt the tiles and knew he was back across, he stood up. He was greeted by the amazed stares of Lori and all the rest of his class.

Lori gave him a hand and helped him climb out. "You sure are swimming, all right. My word, Raymond, you're a regular fish. You were swimming underwater. That was great. Now all you have to do is come on up and swim on the surface. You're going to be a great swimmer, Raymond, just great!"

3

By the last week of lessons every member of Red Team could swim across the pool. Except Raymond. Determined to live up to his teacher's expectations, he swam furiously, morning after morning. He knew he crossed that pool twice as often as anyone else in the class. Across and back, across and back he went. It was so easy by this time that he was always astonished to find himself on the other side before he could get to the surface. He could float as long as his breath held out. But the minute he began to move his arms and legs, he went right under and stayed there.

Lori noticed how hard he was working and tried to help him. She got into the water with him and watched him all the way across. She tried starting him out different ways, even on his back, but he sank as soon as he began to swim, no matter how he started out. Lori held him on the surface, but that didn't do any good either. He simply couldn't make any progress at all unless he was underwater. Nothing seemed to help him swim properly.

Finally Lori told him to quit trying so hard. "Just enjoy yourself," she said.

But Raymond did not want to give up. He worked and worked, hoping that if he crossed the pool often enough, he would surely find himself swimming like everybody else. He went faster and faster; he felt he could hold his breath longer and longer, but nothing helped him swim the normal way.

Lori praised him for trying so hard. "I think you're part porpoise, Raymond," Benjamin said, with real awe in his voice. "You're so fast, Raymond. You're the fastest swimmer of anyone here, I bet."

Raymond appreciated this praise, but he couldn't help feeling that something must be dreadfully wrong with him. At night he dreamed he was swimming. It always seemed, in his dream, that he was about to rise triumphantly to the surface. When he woke up, he would be breathing hard, his blankets all in a tangle.

As the last Friday of lessons approached,

the day the certificates were to be handed out, Raymond actually considered playing sick. Many mothers and fathers would be there. Eloise and her mother would be coming with him and his parents. Benjamin's mother and sisters were driving with Kim and Scott and Mrs. Ellsworth. Raymond's father was actually taking the morning off to come and see him swim. There was no way he could stay home.

Lori told Raymond several times during that last week not to try so hard. "One of these days," she said, "you'll just find yourself swimming along, bingo! Just like that. It will happen someday, Raymond, I'm sure. Probably when you're least expecting it."

"Well," muttered Raymond, "I'm least expecting it right now." Deep inside he had a hope that the last day would be it. He would suddenly be able to swim, really swim. Surely as hard as he was trying, it would happen. It *had* to happen.

Friday morning Eloise and her mother came over early. "Boy," Eloise said as they got into the car, "I can't wait to get my certificate, can you?"

She looked at Raymond, but he didn't say anything. For the rest of the ride he was so busy worrying, he didn't answer any of Eloise's questions or pay any attention to her talk about the next set of swimming lessons they would be able to take the last two weeks of August.

She prattled away about the vacation her family was taking in July, but Raymond wasn't listening. What if he was one of the ones who would have to take the beginning lessons all over again? The rest of the Red

Team would go right on without him and become intermediate swimmers and then swimmers. Why, they would become lifeguards and maybe even racers, and there he'd be, still down there on the bottom of the pool, thrashing around from side to side, getting nowhere.

Glumly he got into his swim trunks and sat beside Benjamin with the others, waiting for Red Team's turn to go through its paces.

By the time it was Red Team's turn, Raymond was completely downcast. The other team members were enthusiastically showing all the steps they had gone through in the process of learning to swim to earn their certificates. Although Raymond joined in everything, his heart wasn't in it.

When the time came to jump in and swim across the pool and back, the final test, Raymond was not surprised when Lori held him back and whispered to him to go sit down a second. He slumped down on the bench, wishing he could suddenly become invisible. This was even worse than he had imagined.

He couldn't bear to watch the others jump in and splash their way across the pool. He looked studiously at his feet, carefully watching trickles of water merge into little pools around his toes. He wished he had never signed up for lessons in the first place. You could probably go all through life without swimming anyway.

Lori told the Red Team members to sit down and put their towels around their shoulders. "Red Team has something to show you this morning," she said after she had blown her whistle for everyone to be quiet. "We have a very special swimmer on our team. Raymond, will you come up now?"

Raymond couldn't believe his ears, but he got up and stood beside Lori. "Raymond has learned to swim in his own way. He may be a porpoise in disguise, he swims underwater so well." She turned to Raymond as everyone, especially the rest of Red Team, laughed delightedly. "You won't mind giving us a demonstration of your underwater ability, will you, Raymond?"

Raymond was speechless, but he looked up at Lori and nodded.

"Okay, folks, here's Red Team's own porpoise. Go for it, Raymond."

With the sound of clapping loud in his ears, Raymond jumped into the water and took off. When he felt the other wall of the pool, he was so full of joy and excitement, he just turned and swam right back to the other side. He felt he could hold his breath forever if needed. He pushed up to find Lori's anxious face looking down at him.

"Why, Raymond!" she cried, helping him out of the pool. "How about that?" she said, turning to the audience. "This is the first time Raymond has ever done both laps! Even I didn't know he could do that."

"Am I going to get my certificate after all?" Raymond asked her as applause rang out.

"Why, Raymond, of course. Of course you'll get your certificate. Did you think you wouldn't?" She gave him a quick hug as she put his towel around his shoulders. "Everyone on my team always passes." She grinned at him as he sat down. "Red Team is one hundred percent all the way. When the next class comes around, you'll find swimming will come naturally to you. Just relax and enjoy the water, Raymond. You've got the makings of a great swimmer."

4

Raymond had been sitting on his front steps for more than an hour. In all that time only one person had passed his house. Doug Sanders, a high school boy who lived two doors down from the Ellsworths, was taking care of several yards in the neighborhood, watering and mowing lawns. He walked by with a leaf rake over his shoulder. The Ellsworths' cat had come across the street to see if Raymond was doing anything interesting. She was sitting beside Raymond on the steps.

"Hi, Raymond, hi, Percolator," Doug said. He stopped to pet the cat and give her a scratch under the chin. "What are you two doing this afternoon?"

"There's nothing to do," complained Raymond. "Everyone's gone."

Eloise and Kim both had left for vacations with their families. Though Raymond and Benjamin had found plenty to do, it did seem strangely quiet without the girls. Then Benjamin, too, had gone away. Mrs. Loftus took him and his sisters on a sudden trip to visit his grandfather, who had gotten sick. For the first time in his life, Raymond found there wasn't enough to keep him busy during the long, quiet days.

Mrs. Wayliss was taking a computer course two mornings a week, and Raymond spent this time happily at the library. Going swimming wasn't much fun without any of his friends. Playing in the backyard wasn't any fun either, all by himself.

"I gotta get a move on. See you later, Percolator," Doug called back as he moved on down the street. Doug was feeding the cat for the Ellsworths while they were gone. He shut the cat in the garage at night and let her out again in the morning.

Presently Percolator, too, went on down the street. Raymond sighed. He had gotten a new book at the library that morning, all about sharks and whales, but he had already looked it over while he waited for his mother. He was looking forward to reading more of it with his father in the evening, but that was long and lonely hours away. He sighed again.

He sat a while longer, thinking it would be a good idea to go inside and get some cold apple juice or get his mother to make lemonade with real lemons. Or it would be even better if the ice-cream truck would drive by and he could get a grapesicle.

The truck that eventually came around the corner, though, didn't sell ice cream. It was a bigger blue truck, with a sign on the side in black letters. Raymond didn't pay much attention to it until it turned into the Ellsworths' drive and parked by the back door. A short hedge separated the Ellsworths' drive from the drive of their neighbors to the left. Two men got out of the truck and opened the back, where a third man had been riding. All three of them were wearing dark blue coveralls. Two men went to the

Ellsworths' back door while the third one went around the hedge to their neighbor's back door.

Idly Raymond watched them. They would soon find out that no one was home at either place. Maybe they were delivering something. Maybe they would come over and ask him if they could leave packages with the Waylisses the way the mailman sometimes did. Perhaps he should go over and tell them no one was home.

But while he was making up his mind, he was surprised to see all three of the men disappear into the two houses. Really interested now, he sat up to watch more closely. Presently the two men came out of the Ellsworths' house, carrying the electric clothes dryer between them. They loaded it into the back of the truck and went back into the house. Soon they came out again with the washer. They disappeared again. This time, when they came out, each man was carrying a television set. Raymond knew the bigger set was from the Ellsworths' family room and the smaller one from the kitchen. The man who had gone into the other house had not come out yet.

Raymond walked across the street and stood by the back of the truck until the two men emerged from the house once more. One was carrying Mrs. Ellsworth's sewing machine, and the other one had the family's computer.

"What are you doing?" Raymond asked politely.

"Scram, kid, you're in the way," the man with the sewing machine said.

Raymond started to deny indignantly that

he was in anyone's way. After all, he was just standing there by the back of the truck not doing a thing.

But the second man said, "We are taking these appliances in for repair, sonny."

"The Ellsworths are away on vacation," Raymond said.

"Yeah, we know." The man slid the computer into the truck and gave Raymond a very friendly smile. "That's right. And we'll have everything fixed and in order by the time they get back. That's the whole idea."

The first man scowled angrily at Raymond and then said to his companion, "We don't have time to yak with kids. Come on." He had a deep and growly voice. He didn't seem to be a nice man at all. He turned at the Ellsworths' back door and glared at Raymond. "Get outta here, kid, and mind your own business."

Raymond had started to back away when the third man came out of the Ellsworths' neighbor's house, carrying a big table lamp. "I'm ready for you now, Les," he said.

"Is that lamp broken, too?" asked Raymond.

The man, startled, almost dropped the lamp. Then he saw Raymond, and sounding as unfriendly as the first man, he growled, "What are you doing here?"

Raymond backed away. "I was just watching."

"Well, get outta here," he ordered. He made a move toward Raymond and looked so threatening that Raymond hurried back across the street.

When repairmen came to the Wayliss home to fix something Mr. Wayliss said he couldn't handle, like the time the dishwasher had backed up and flooded the kitchen, they were always very nice to Raymond. They let him watch and answered all his questions as they worked. The dishwasher repairman joked with Raymond and told Mrs. Wayliss when he left that next time something happened, Raymond could probably fix it for her.

Raymond walked back to his house. "This sure has been a lousy day," he muttered to himself. You couldn't even watch a truck being loaded. Disgustedly he sat down again. At least no one could tell him to go away from his own front steps.

5

Raymond continued to watch the activity across the street. It seemed like a good idea to have things fixed while you were away on a trip. His father often complained that there was always something around the house that needed fixing. But as Raymond watched the men coming and going in and out of the two houses, he began to wonder why so many things had broken at the same time. His mother always said everything seemed to go wrong at once, but Raymond could remember only one time, when the TV wouldn't go on and the toaster blew out the same morning.

He got up and went to the end of his block, crossed the street, and, after walking behind the houses, approached Kim's house from the back. Peering out carefully from behind a rhododendron bush, he saw the friendly man come out with a toaster in one hand and a small transistor radio in the other. He had the electric wall clock tucked under his arm as well.

Since this was the man who had explained to him about the repairs, Raymond was just going to step out and ask him why so many things at the Ellsworths' needed fixing when the first man came out right behind him. He still looked mean. His hands were also full of things. Raymond stood still and watched, completely puzzled now.

There were some very strange things put into that truck from the two houses. The longer he watched, the more peculiar it seemed. Typewriters, clocks, lamps, even two fancy ten-speed bicycles, plus a great many things Raymond couldn't identify.

Raymond studied the letters on the side of the truck until he made out what it spelled. "L and L Repairs." He certainly wished he could ask the friendly repairman a few questions. He was dying to know what was wrong with all these things. Well, it would be nice for the Ellsworths and their neighbors to come home and find everything fixed and working right again, he thought.

When the truck finally drove away, Raymond went back to his own house. His mother was absorbed in her computer lesson for the next day. When he began to tell her about the three men in the repair truck, she said, "Hmmmm, what's that, Raymond?"

He started to explain again, but he could see her mind was on the computer, so he turned away. "I'll tell you later."

"Fine, hon," she said.

Raymond went back outside, deep in thought. Maybe he would go find Doug and talk to him. Somehow he felt a need to tell someone about what he had seen. He wandered around the neighborhood awhile, but Doug either had finished for the day or was working somewhere else. Finally he went back home and got out his library book. Soon he was immersed in the world of sharks, completely forgetting about everything else.

That evening at the dinner table he had

just begun to tell his parents about the repairmen and their big van when the doorbell
rang. It was Doug, a very excited Doug.

"Hey, Mr. Wayliss," he began breathlessly,
"do you think I should call the police? I was
just at the Ellsworths' feeding the cat, and
everything's gone. I mean, when I went into
the utility room to get a new sack of cat food,
it was empty. I mean, not the cat food, the
washer and dryer, even the iron and the iron-
ing board, I mean, they were just gone."

"Slow down, Doug," Mr. Wayliss said when
Doug had to stop to draw a breath.

Raymond seized this opportunity to break
in. "I was just telling you. A repair truck
came and took them away. The men said
they'd have them all fixed and back by the
time the Ellsworths come home from their
vacation."

"Oh," said Doug, "that's what happened. Oh, okay then." He was very relieved.

Raymond went on. "They took the TVs, too, and the big clock and the transistor and the computer. Oh, they took a lot of things to fix."

"What, what?" cried Doug and Mr. Wayliss and Mrs. Wayliss all at the same time.

"I've been trying to tell you. A big truck drove up. There were three men, and I went over to watch. One of them told me to leave and get out of the way, but another one said they were taking the things to fix and would have them all back by the time the Ellsworths get back from their trip. And I wasn't in the way; I was just standing there watching. I wanted to know why so many things needed fixing. They sure had a lot of things that were busted, I guess. And they took a lot of stuff from the house next door, too."

"What!" Raymond's three listeners cried again.

"I'll call the police," Mr. Wayliss said to Doug.

"Good grief," Mrs. Wayliss said.

Doug said eagerly, "Should I go over and check and see what else is gone?"

"No, no, you wait here. We'll let the police do the checking," Mr. Wayliss said from the telephone.

"I can tell you," Raymond said. "I went around the corner and watched from behind a bush."

"Raymond, you didn't!" gasped Mrs. Wayliss. "They might have hurt you."

"They didn't see me," said Raymond. "I was going to ask the nice one how come so many things got broken all at once, that's all. But I never could; the other two were always around. They were mean, those two."

"Oh, my goodness, Raymond," Mrs. Wayliss said. She gave him a hug. "Why didn't you tell me sooner?" Before Raymond could reply, she went on. "Oh, I was doing my lesson, wasn't I? Oh, dear, oh, dear."

6

The whole evening was a very exciting one. First two policemen came, and Mr. Wayliss and Doug went across the street with them. Raymond wanted to go, too, but his mother wouldn't let him. Soon, though, they came back, and the policemen wanted to talk to Raymond.

"I understand you're the one who saw these guys loading up their truck. Can you tell us about it?"

Raymond could and he did. He talked so fast, the policemen asked him to slow down so they could make notes. They asked him lots of questions. What color was the truck? What did it say on the side? How many things did Raymond see them putting in the truck? What exactly did they say to him? What did each of them look like?

He couldn't tell much about the unfriendly two, except that they looked and acted mean. "But the other one," he said, "had light brown hair and real blue eyes and a crooked tooth up front when he smiled and lots of curly hair on his hands and wrists."

"Did you by any chance hear them calling each other any name at all?" asked the policeman when Raymond had finally told them all he could remember. "Think carefully now. That could help us identify them."

Raymond shook his head. "They didn't talk

to each other much. They were busy, and they just grunted a lot. Oh yes. I forgot. When the one came out of the other house, not the Ellsworths'—"

"Singleton. That's the Singletons' house," his mother broke in to say.

"Well," Raymond continued, "well, when he came out carrying that big lamp, he said, 'I'm ready for you, Les.'"

"You sure it was Les?"

Raymond nodded.

"I don't suppose you happened to notice what the license plate was?" asked the other policeman, looking up from the notebook he was busy writing in.

"Oh yes," Raymond said. "The number was just one more than Grandma's street number. It was XXT three-six-eight-one. Grandma's address is three-six-eight-oh."

Both policemen were ever so pleased with that. Chuckling, the first said, "Young man, you're just about the best witness I've ever come across."

And the other one said, "Fantastic! If we don't catch these burglars, I'll have to turn in my badge."

The police drove away after thanking Raymond several times. "Will you get the Ellsworths' things back?" asked Raymond as they were leaving.

"Well, if we don't, it's sure not your fault." They had already gotten a phone number for the Ellsworths from Doug and said they would be contacting them. Mrs. Wayliss told them where the Singletons' son lived so they could let them know, too.

"I hope you don't have to turn in your badge," Raymond said seriously as the two policemen went out the door.

They both laughed. "Don't you worry about that, sonny. You've been the kind of help we don't get very often. We'll sure try to make this a quick one."

Doug stayed on to talk awhile. He, too, was very impressed with Raymond. "Gee," he said, "you might be in the papers again. Maybe on TV. You were great."

"I don't want Raymond in the papers over this," Mrs. Wayliss said. "You never know what might happen. If these guys find out it was Raymond who—" She stopped, shuddering.

"He might have to identify these guys," Doug said eagerly. "In a lineup, like on TV. But they won't see him," he said hastily after a look at Mrs. Wayliss.

She turned to Mr. Wayliss. "Do you think

we should ask them not to mention Raymond's name?"

"Don't worry. I'll ask them about it. Meanwhile"—he turned to Raymond and Doug—"let's kind of keep it to ourselves for a day or two, okay?"

7

The policemen returned the very next day. They had some pictures of men they wanted Raymond to look at. They told Mrs. Wayliss not to worry, Raymond's name would not be in the paper. "Thanks to your son here, I'm sure we'll be able to catch up with these guys very soon. But they'll never know about Raymond. Don't give it another thought, Mrs. Wayliss."

As soon as Doug saw the police car in front of the Wayliss house, he rushed right over to see if he could be of help. Raymond was just beginning to sort through the pictures. Carefully Raymond looked at each of the faces in the photographs. Then he shook his head. "I don't see any of the robbers here. I'm sorry."

"Well, we can't have good luck every time, Raymond," said the policeman.

He had gathered up the photos, preparing to leave, when Doug asked eagerly, "Did you find out about the license number?"

The policemen looked at each other. One shrugged, and the other one said, "I guess you deserve to hear about it. We found it was a plate stolen last year from a used-car lot in Lynnwood." He turned to Mrs. Wayliss. "Your neighbors will be back in a couple of days. Thanks to Raymond here, we hope we'll have the thieves rounded up before they've had a chance to get rid of any of the stuff."

"What if they just drove it off to another state?" asked Doug. He was practically bursting with excitement at being involved in this affair.

"That's a strong possibility," the policeman said. "But we've alerted all the neighboring departments to be on the lookout. Robberies like this generally rely on a very quick turnover of the goods, so it's most likely they headed for someplace in the city.

"There have been quite a few of these vacation thefts over in Edmonds and Bellevue in the past few years. This is a good chance to break up a ring that's pretty well organized. Burglaries like this aren't just the work of some random small-time operator. They take a lot of arranging beforehand and plenty of planning. It will be a great break for us if we can trace these things before they're all disposed of."

"Do you think you can get the Ellsworths' TV and stuff back before they get home?" asked Raymond.

"We're sure going to try, son. Maybe their stuff won't be back in the house, but we sure hope that we can have good news for them and eventually they'll get everything back."

"They can come and watch TV with us till then, can't they, Mom?" Raymond looked anxiously at his mother.

The policemen laughed, and Mrs. Wayliss smiled at her son. "Of course, Raymond. We'll do everything we can to help them out."

"Boy," Doug said as the police left, "I sure

hope they catch those guys. It's going to be an awful shock to the Ellsworths. You should see their place. It looks so *bare!*"

"They're so lucky you were taking care of their cat and found out so soon about the robbery," said Mrs. Wayliss.

"Yeah, but it was Raymond who saw it all."

"I was looking for you that day," Raymond said. "I was going to ask you about everything breaking at once. I wondered about that."

"It was only a couple of hours before I went there myself. Well, I gotta go get to work. Keep your eyes open, Raymond."

Raymond promised that he would.

The Singletons arrived home first and came over to the Waylisses' to discuss the robbery. Several hours later the Ellsworths drove up. Raymond was sitting on his front steps, keeping a lookout. He wanted to rush right over, but Mrs. Wayliss said he should wait and let the Ellsworths unpack and get over the first shock by themselves. To Raymond's satisfaction it wasn't long before all the Ellsworths came across the street.

"Oh, what an awful thing to happen," Mrs. Wayliss said as she came out the door to greet their neighbors.

"The police seem to think we stand a very good chance of getting everything back," Mr. Ellsworth said. "They told us that thanks to Raymond, they hope to bust up a big ring of robbers in this area." All the Ellsworth family looked at Raymond approvingly. Scott, Kim's little brother, smiled at Raymond, and Kim looked at him, her big brown eyes shining.

The rest of the week was very exciting. The Singletons also said how much they appreciated the help Raymond had given the police. They said it was nice to live in a neighborhood where people looked out for each other and how proud the Waylisses must be of their son.

Kim went to the library with Raymond on his mother's class days, and Mrs. Ellsworth took Raymond to the swimming pool when Kim and Scott went. It was very pleasant to have someone to do things with again.

Just when Mrs. Ellsworth said she was getting awfully tired of taking the family laundry out to the Laundromat, the Ellsworths got the good news from the police that their household things had been re-covered.

"We'll get to have everything back real soon," Kim reported. "And the Singletons, too. Daddy went down to identify our stuff with Mr. Singleton. Daddy said stuff was there we hadn't even missed yet."

That evening, once again a police car drove up to the Waylisses'. Doug had just come by to rejoice in the good news. It was the same two officers who had come the first time. They both had big smiles on their faces.

Kim and Raymond had been working on a new puzzle Kim had brought back from her trip. They had spread the pieces out on the kitchen table. It was a really difficult puzzle with lots of pieces. Doug came out to the kitchen to get them.

"The police want to see you, Raymond. I guess they're going to tell us all about it. Should I run over and get the Ellsworths?" he asked the policemen as he came back to the front room with Kim and Raymond. "They'll want to hear it, too." He dashed out without waiting for an answer, calling back, "And I'll get the Singletons, too."

So there was quite an audience gathered at the Wayliss house when the police told their story. "It's all because of our helper here," the first one began, smiling at Raymond. "He watched and remembered so well, we've been able to track down a big gang of thieves. They specialized in exactly what Raymond saw them doing across the street. Thanks to his alertness, we were able to round up the whole operation before they had disposed of this last load. A lot of other folks are going to get things back, too. You've made a bunch of people happy, Raymond."

"Is he going to get a reward?" Doug burst in.

"I'm sure we all think he deserves one," the policeman answered. "Our chief has authorized us to present this to you, Raymond, in appreciation of all your assistance."

He gave Raymond a piece of paper. It was like the certificate he got at swimming lessons, only it was thicker paper and had fancier lettering.

"Let everyone hear what it says." The policeman took the paper back from Raymond and, after clearing his throat, read, "'The Department of Law and Order of the Municipality of Kenton confers upon Raymond Arthur Wayliss the status of honorary police officer in gratitude for his aid and support.' It is signed by His Honor the Mayor and the chief of police."

Everyone cheered and clapped. Doug said he still thought Raymond should get a reward, but Raymond himself was very pleased and satisfied. He looked at the paper in his hands. Honorary policeman. That was reward enough.

Life at Raymond's house seemed pretty quiet after all the excitement died down. Raymond's mother took him to the store, where they bought a frame for the certificate, and his father hung it in his room. At first Raymond looked at it often and with great pleasure, but presently it seemed like part of the furnishings, and he seldom gave it more than a passing glance, happy as he was with it.

Just when Raymond began to sigh and wish that Benjamin would hurry up and come home, something wonderful happened.

Grandma Wayliss called from San Francisco. Raymond answered the phone.

"You're the very one I wanted to talk to," she said. "Think you have time to come down and see me?" Before he could answer, she went right on. "Put your mother on the phone, Raymond. I'm going to make her an offer she can't resist. And I have a surprise for you, one I know you'll love."

"Okay, I'll get Mom. Are you sending me something?"

"Oh, it's better than that, Raymond. Much better."

Raymond listened impatiently while his mother talked to his grandmother. The minute she put down the phone, his questions burst out. "Can we go? What did she say? When can we go?"

Even as he asked all these questions, Raymond knew the answers. His mother was smiling broadly.

"Slow down, give me a chance." She laughed. "I'll have to call your father, but I wouldn't be at all surprised if we find we can have a little vacation after all."

Mr. Wayliss readily agreed that Grandma's offer was too good to turn down. By the very next day it was all settled. Grandma's surprise was to pay for Raymond's ticket to fly down to San Francisco if his parents could manage to come along. She told Raymond's mother there were more surprises to come, but she wouldn't say what they were. "You'll find out when you get here," Grandma said again.

It was Raymond's first chance to travel by air, and he liked everything about it. The two hours from Seattle to San Francisco were all too short.

After allowing Grandma to kiss him at the airport, Raymond said eagerly, "Are you going to tell me your surprise now, Grandma?" They were going down the long escalator to the baggage claim. Grandma was just behind Raymond, so he was talking to her over his shoulder.

"Raymond," his father said, "watch your step."

Raymond turned his head around just as it was his turn to step off. He took Grandma's hand. She looked down at him with a big smile. "Yes, Raymond, you've waited long enough. My friend Millie Burgess has been wanting me to drive down with her to Monterey to see the famous aquarium there. I told her I'd go if you could come down and go with us. How about that? It's quite new, and people say it's a wonderful place."

"Oh yes," cried Raymond. "I really like aquariums. Do you think they have a shark?"

Grandma laughed. "They have a sample of all the sea life found in Monterey Bay, I understand, but I don't know about sharks. I do know there will be lots and lots to see, and your parents can have a couple of days by themselves while we're gone," Grandma continued. "So we're all going to have a fine time, aren't we?"

10

It was indeed a splendid week. There was so much to do before the trip to Monterey that they were busy every single moment. Even the weather cooperated. Grandma said such clear skies hadn't been seen in the city all summer.

Finally the great day came. The moment he stepped into the Monterey aquarium, Raymond's expectations were fulfilled. The very first thing he saw was his old friend, the great blue whale, life size, suspended over his head, with its smaller relatives around it. This was part of a special whale exhibit, and Raymond could have spent the entire day right there.

Millie Burgess told Grandma she was very impressed at how much Raymond knew about the deep-sea creatures. "Oh, Raymond soaks up facts like a sponge," Grandma said proudly.

It was true that much of the information describing the displays was already known to Raymond, but that made it all the more wonderful. It was like visiting with old friends.

Raymond went slowly from exhibit to exhibit, savoring every moment. There was a giant whale puzzle to assemble; unhesitatingly Raymond fitted the pieces together.

When Grandma read him the questions on the true/false test about whales, he could answer correctly almost before the question was finished. This was all familiar stuff from his reading with his father.

"Isn't this fun?" he said, beaming.

"Oh, Grandma, can we do this?" "This" was an exhibit labeled "The Whale Trail." Visitors were supposed to go past five different stations and, with a big stamp, press onto a card the answers to questions asked about a different whale at each stop. If you didn't know the correct answer immediately, there were two clues given to help you choose. Grandma read the question out to Raymond at the first stop, and he didn't need the clues to know which whale was the right one to stamp on his card.

"Don't tell us, Raymond." Millie laughed.

"We'll see if we can do it as well as you." She and Grandma took cards and stamped their answers in the proper square. If you got the correct answer, an ink-blue picture of that whale appeared with its name.

The first question was: "Which whale is the biggest?" Since there were many pictures and exhibits about the gigantic size of this creature, Millie and Grandma got that answer right the first time.

Though Raymond knew every whale immediately, Grandma and Millie both missed on "Which whale composes songs and is known as the singing whale?" So on their cards, instead of the picture of a humpback whale, they got the message "Wrong. Try again." This made them laugh.

They progressed down the whole trail, answering questions about the gray whale, the sperm whale, and the orca or killer whale. Raymond didn't miss a single one. Then he got another card and stamped it for Benjamin.

He wanted to go back to the start of the whale exhibit and look at everything again, especially the part at the beginning that was about the great blue whale: "The biggest animal that ever lived, as big as four dinosaurs, as big as 350 cows, as big as 2,000 people."

There was a picture of a blue whale beside four huge dinosaurs. There was a small model of the whale beside numerous small plastic cows mounted beside it. There was an enormous blowup of a picture of two thousand people standing packed tightly together. And stretching over it all, the great body of the blue whale reaching from one end of the whole whale exhibit to the other!

11

Raymond thought the whale exhibit was
the very best thing in the whole aquarium,
even after he had seen everything else. Still,
he also fell in love with the sea otters, especially at feeding time, and he couldn't get
enough of the big tank full of so many kinds
of fish swimming about.

He stayed so long at the Touch and Feel
pool and asked so many good questions that
the young woman who explained about all

the creatures there told him she would like to keep him as her helper.

There were places where you could look down into the water and then go down and look up and into the water exactly as if you were a fish yourself. Grandma and Millie had to go sit down and rest while Raymond ran up and down several times to do this.

At first he was disappointed when the ladies bypassed the cafeteria over in one corner of the aquarium to go to the dining room. But when they were seated by a window looking out over the bay, where some big seals lay basking in the sun on the rocks and several kinds of birds—cormorants, sea gulls, and pelicans— were all in view, Raymond forgot the good smells of hamburgers and french fries.

He was made even happier when the waiter brought them two little brown loaves of bread, each baked in the shape of a whale flipping its tail perkily. He set one down in front of Raymond, saying, "You look as if you might be hungry enough to eat a whale all by yourself."

Before the day was over, there was time to look at all the things for sale in the aquarium gift shop. Grandma bought Raymond a sea-green T-shirt with a big grouper on it. He looked carefully until he found just what he wanted for each one of his friends.

For Benjamin, he chose a pen with a section full of seawater with tiny starfish floating in it. He found a tiny pin shaped like a baby seal for Eloise. He picked a jar of the tiniest shells for Kim. It would add a lot to her shell collection.

In the late afternoon both Grandma and Millie said they needed to sit down. "You won't mind going around by yourself a bit, will you? There are guards posted all around, I notice."

"'Course not." Raymond laughed. "You couldn't get lost here."

So while the women sat in the rest area that looked out across the big deck from which you could watch the little sea creatures in the tidal pools, Raymond went back to the Touch and Feel pool, the kelp forest, the seafloor exhibit, and the whale show.

"Well, Raymond," Grandma said as the closing bell sounded and a voice over the intercom said the aquarium was closing its doors for the day, "did you see everything?"

"Oh, yes," Raymond replied happily. "But if I lived here, I'd come every day. Maybe I'd even get a job here. I think it would be fun to work here. I'd like to help take care of the fish."

When Raymond shut his eyes that night, it seemed as if all the bright-colored fish he had seen that day were swimming right there behind his eyeballs. It was a fine sight to see.

After breakfast the next morning Millie told Raymond he could have one last swim. Raymond had the sparkling blue pool all to himself. He pretended he was a spouting whale for a while, coming up for air and spraying water as far up as he could. He swam lazily about, splashing as much as he liked, rolling over, ducking down, and generally having a wonderful time.

The pool was oval-shaped and not large, so

it was no challenge to swim across it. He decided to start at the steps and swim all around the pool, keeping close to the edge. He had nearly made it when suddenly he realized he was swimming on the surface of the water. It had finally happened, just as Lori said it would.

He let out a whoop of joy. "Grandma, Grandma," he called. "Millie, come see. I'm swimming, I'm swimming!"

Both of them came running. "What is it?" "What's the matter?"

"I can swim." He launched himself across the pool and then swam back. "See, I'm swimming."

"Well, of course you are. You've been swimming all along," Grandma said.

"But only underwater. Now I can stay up. Now I can *really* swim." And off he swam again to show them.

All the long drive back to San Francisco, Raymond thought about telling everyone he had finally learned to swim. He could barely wait to tell them when he had a thought that was even better. He wouldn't tell them. He'd show them! The last summer session of swimming lessons was due to start when he returned home. He'd wait and give everyone a big surprise.

For a while it had looked as if it were going to be a long and draggy summer. Now when he got back, everyone else would have returned, and boy! what a lot he and Kim had to tell them. She would let him tell it, too. He had to admit she was pretty nice that way. It was going to make Eloise's eyes pop right out when she saw his certificate from the police department.

Grandma turned from the front seat to look at him. "Everything okay?" she asked.

"Oh, yes," said Raymond. "Oh, yes. I was just thinking. You know what, Grandma?"

"No, what, "Raymond?"

"I've been thinking, and I think this is the best summer I ever had in my whole life!" Grandma chuckled. "And you know what else, Grandma?"

"No, what else?"

"School starts again pretty soon. I'll be in second grade. It's going to be great."

"Is this the Raymond I once knew who was never going to school?" Grandma Wayliss laughed.

"Oh," Raymond protested, "that was way back when I was little. I didn't know so much then. It's going to be great," Raymond repeated. "I can't wait."